GEORGE O'CONN

APHRODITE

GODDESS OF LOVE

A NEAL PORTER BOOK

New York

IN THE TIME BEFORE TIME,
THERE WAS NOTHING, KAOS.

FROM OUT OF KAOS CAME GE,
OR GAEA, OUR MOTHER EARTH.

BUT SHE WAS NOT ALONE.

WHEN KAOS BROUGHT FORTH GAEA, ANOTHER ENTITY CAME INTO THE COSMOS.
A DESIRE FOR COMPANIONSHIP, A DESIRE TO CREATE NEW LIFE THAT SUFFUSED THE EMPTINESS THAT SURROUNDED YOUNG GAEA.
THE LOVE BETWEEN EARTH AND SKY WAS VIOLENT AND UNPREDICTABLE. TUMULTUOUS.

NOT QUITE A GOD, NOT EVEN QUITE A BEING, BUT MORE OF A FORCE, A POWER.
EROS, THE POWER OF LOVE.
NOW AWARE OF HER LONELINESS, GAEA DESIRED COMPANIONSHIP, AND CREATED THE SKY, OURANOS.
EROS WAS A YOUNG POWER THEN, WITH NO CENTER, NO FOCUS; BUT STILL, IT WAS PRESENT, FUELING THEIR PASSION.
IN TIME, SOME OF THE ESSENCE OF EARTH AND SKY MIXED, COMBINED, AND NEW LIFE WAS BROUGHT FORTH.

THE FIRST CHILDREN OF EARTH AND SKY WERE THE TITANS, THE GODS OF TIME.
THEY WERE FOLLOWED BY THE HEKATONCHIERES, WITH THEIR FIFTY HEADS AND ONE HUNDRED HANDS.
AND THE ONE-EYED CYCLOPES, AS POWERFUL AS STORMS.
EROS BROUGHT OTHER THINGS BESIDES LOVE TO THE COSMOS.
LIKE JEALOUSY, WHICH OURANOS NOW FELT.
PREVIOUSLY HE HAD HAD THE LOVE OF GAEA ALL TO HIMSELF, BUT NOW HER LOVE WAS SHARED AMONG THEIR CHILDREN.
DEEP, DEEP IN GRANDMOTHER EARTH WAS TARTAROS, A PLACE SO DEEP THAT EROS HAD BEEN UNABLE TO PERMEATE IT.
OURANOS SPLIT OPEN GAEA AND IMPRISONED THE HEKATONCHIERES AND CYCLOPES DEEP IN THE DARK OF TARTAROS.
FEWER CHILDREN TO SHARE THE LOVE OF GRANDMOTHER EARTH.
AND WITH LOVE, WITH JEALOUSY, CAME HATE.
AND NOW EARTH HATED THE SKY.

GAEA HAD A PLAN.
SHE WHISPERED SWEET NOTHINGS TO OURANOS, AND BROUGHT HIM CLOSE TO HER.
HE DIDN'T SEE KRONOS, THE YOUNGEST OF THE TITANS, APPROACH, ARMED WITH A SICKLE OF UNBREAKABLE ADAMANTINE.
DEEP WITHIN OURANOS WAS THE PLACE WHERE THE POWER OF EROS HAD ITS SEAT, WHERE IT FUELED HIS LOVE, HIS PASSION AND DESIRE.
AND KRONOS CUT IT AWAY.

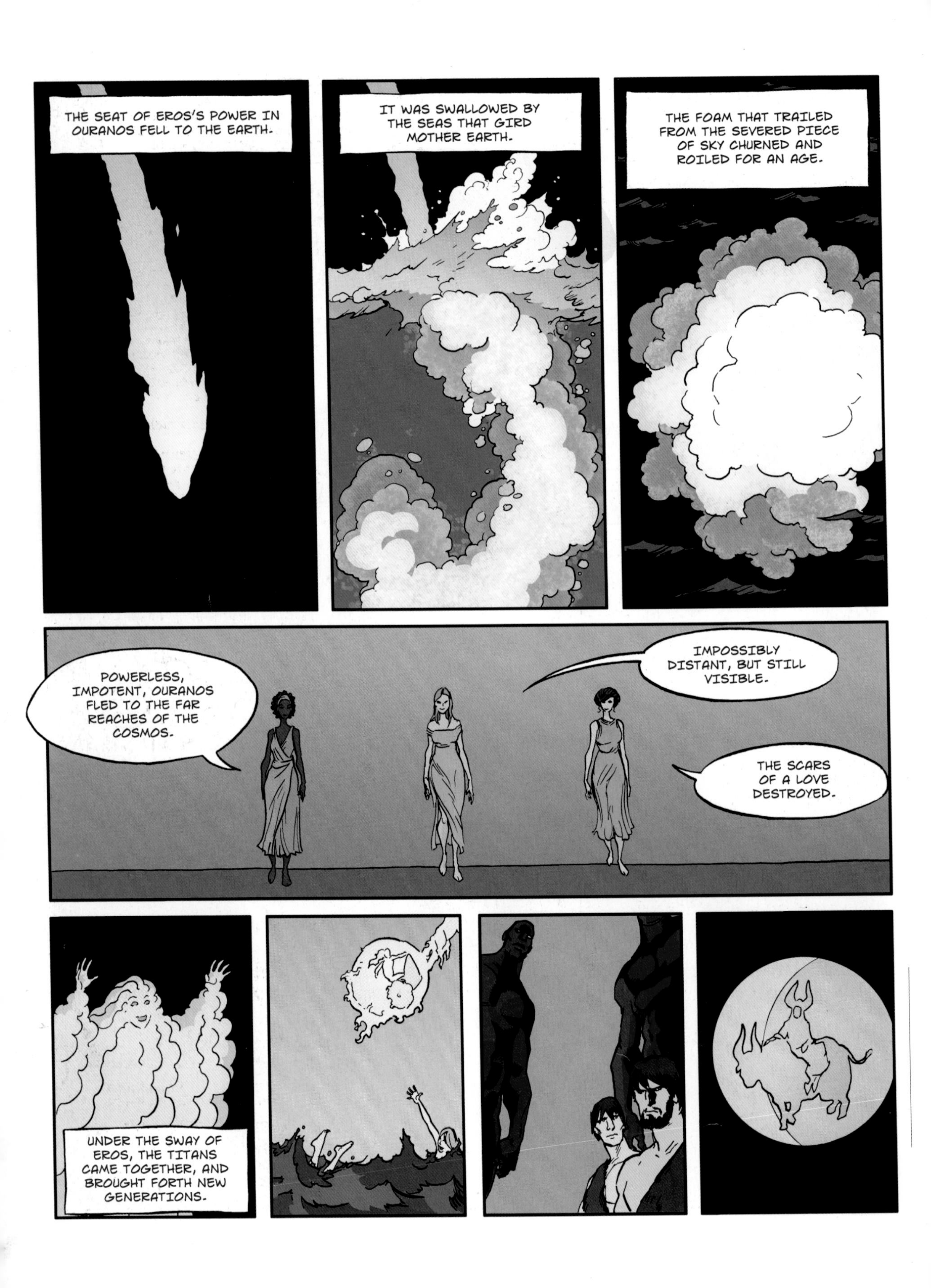
THE SEAT OF EROS'S POWER IN OURANOS FELL TO THE EARTH.
IT WAS SWALLOWED BY THE SEAS THAT GIRD MOTHER EARTH.
THE FOAM THAT TRAILED FROM THE SEVERED PIECE OF SKY CHURNED AND ROILED FOR AN AGE.
POWERLESS, IMPOTENT, OURANOS FLED TO THE FAR REACHES OF THE COSMOS.
IMPOSSIBLY DISTANT, BUT STILL VISIBLE.
THE SCARS OF A LOVE DESTROYED.
UNDER THE SWAY OF EROS, THE TITANS CAME TOGETHER, AND BROUGHT FORTH NEW GENERATIONS.

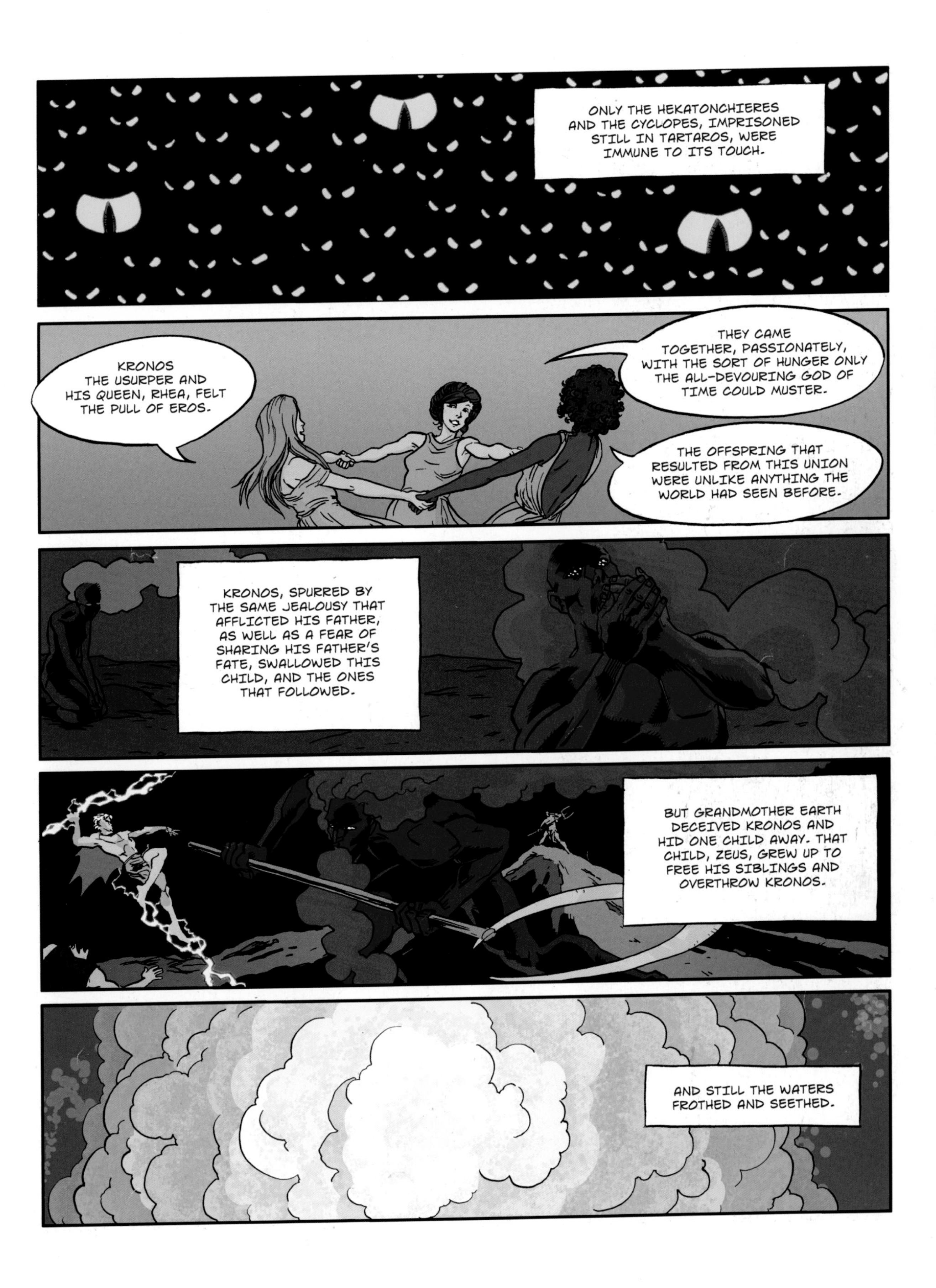
ONLY THE HEKATONCHIERES AND THE CYCLOPES, IMPRISONED STILL IN TARTAROS, WERE IMMUNE TO ITS TOUCH.
KRONOS THE USURPER AND HIS QUEEN, RHEA, FELT THE PULL OF EROS.
THEY CAME TOGETHER, PASSIONATELY, WITH THE SORT OF HUNGER ONLY THE ALL-DEVOURING GOD OF TIME COULD MUSTER.
THE OFFSPRING THAT RESULTED FROM THIS UNION WERE UNLIKE ANYTHING THE WORLD HAD SEEN BEFORE.
KRONOS, SPURRED BY THE SAME JEALOUSY THAT AFFLICTED HIS FATHER, AS WELL AS A FEAR OF SHARING HIS FATHER'S FATE, SWALLOWED THIS CHILD, AND THE ONES THAT FOLLOWED.
BUT GRANDMOTHER EARTH DECEIVED KRONOS AND HID ONE CHILD AWAY. THAT CHILD, ZEUS, GREW UP TO FREE HIS SIBLINGS AND OVERTHROW KRONOS.
AND STILL THE WATERS FROTHED AND SEETHED.

ZEUS AND THESE NEW GODS, THE OLYMPIANS, WERE NO STRANGERS TO EROS'S POWER.
THEY COUPLED WITH ONE ANOTHER, WITH OTHER BEINGS, WITH MONSTERS, EVEN WITH HUMANS.
AND IN TURN, THEY PRODUCED MORE GODS, MORE HEROES, MORE MONSTERS...
ALL ACROSS THE EARTH, THERE WAS AN AMAZING VARIETY OF LIFE, ALL UNDER THE SWAY, THE PASSION, THE GENERATIVE POWER OF EROS.

STILL WITHOUT A FOCUS, OR A CENTER, OR A GUIDING INTELLIGENCE. BUT EVERYWHERE, AND WITHIN EVERYONE.
THEN, ONE DAY, THE SWIRLING FROTH THAT SEETHED AND SIMMERED FROM THE SEVERED PORTION OF OURANOS, THE PORTION THAT HAD HOUSED HIS OWN EROS—
—CREATED A MIND FOR ITSELF.
AND, SUDDENLY, EROS WAS AWARE.
SHE SHAPED THE WATER AND FOAM ABOUT HER INTO A PERFECT PHYSICAL FORM.
DO YOU REMEMBER THAT DAY, SISTERS? I DOUBT ANY WHO LIVED THEN COULD EVER FORGET, WOULD EVER *WANT* TO FORGET.

THE POWER OF EROS,
GIVEN FLESH AT LAST.

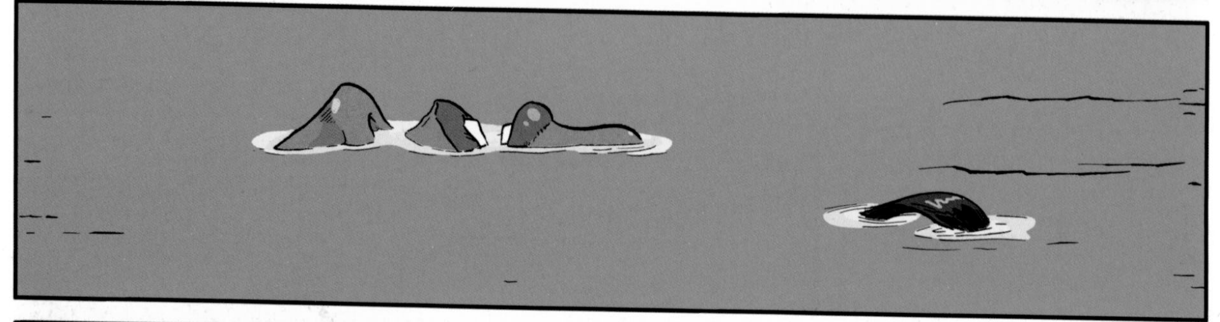

SHE HEADED TOWARD THE
SHORE OF THE NEAREST
ISLAND, CALLED CYPRUS.

IT WAS ZEPHYROS, THE WEST WIND, WHO FIRST SPOTTED HER. HE BLEW HER SWEET FRAGRANCE OVER THE LANDS NEAR AND FAR.
SHE SMILED, LAUGHING AS THE WIND TOUSLED HER NEWBORN HAIR.
EVERYTHING IN THE WORLD WANTED TO PLEASE HER.
THE WATER THAT COATED HER BODY DIDN'T WANT TO LEAVE HER. IT RECONFIGURED ITSELF, TRANSFORMED ITSELF INTO SPARKLING SILKS AND FLOWING FABRICS.
HER PERFECTLY FORMED FEET TOUCHED THE EARTH, AND WILD FLOWERS SPRANG UP IN ECSTATIC EBULLIENCE OF NEW LIFE.

AND THIS WAS HOW THE WORLD MET APHRODITE.

WE WERE THERE THEN, SISTERS.
WE, WHO TRAFFICKED IN BEAUTY, IN CHARM, IN GRACE.
AND EVEN WE WERE STRUCK DUMB.
SO GREAT WAS HER ALLURE WE PLEDGED OURSELVES TO HER THAT VERY MOMENT.
WE, THE THREE CHARITES, ATTENDANTS OF APHRODITE.
AGLAIA...
EUPHROSYNE...
AND THALIA.

THE POWER OF EROS HAD EXISTED BEFORE, SINCE THE TIME BEFORE TIME.
BUT NOW, FOR THE FIRST TIME, IT HAD A CONSCIOUSNESS, AN AVATAR.
ALL THINGS EVERYWHERE FELT THE STIRRINGS OF LOVE.
DEEP, DEEP DOWN, IN THE REALM OF HADES, THE GOD WHO SHARED THAT NAME LOOKED SKYWARD, AS SURELY AS IF HE HAD BEEN CALLED, BUT NO ONE HAD SPOKEN HIS NAME.
DEEPER STILL, IN TARTAROS, THE TITANS STOPPED STRUGGLING AGAINST THEIR ADAMANTINE PRISON, THE IMPENETRABLE DARKNESS PENETRATED BY EROS AT LAST.
AND FAR AWAY, ON OLYMPUS, THE HOME OF THE GODS...

ZEUS, KING OF GODS AND MEN, AND THE OLYMPIAN MOST ATTUNED TO THE TOUCH OF EROS, FELT IT FIRST.
WHAT
ON
EARTH
IS
THAT?!
EVEN THOSE WHO HAD NEVER SUCCUMBED TO THE POWER OF EROS FELT A STIRRING.
THE EYES OF AN OLYMPIAN ARE NOT LIKE YOURS OR MINE.
THERE. ON CYPRUS.

THE EYES OF AN OLYMPIAN CAN SEE WHAT THEY WANT, WHAT THEY NEED TO SEE.
I SEE IT.
AND I'LL SEE YOU GUYS THERE!
LIKE HADES, YOU WILL!
OOF!
BOYS!
BOYS!
I DON'T UNDERSTAND THEM.
WE'LL ALL GO DOWN TO CYPRUS TOGETHER.
WAIT FOR ME!
YOU LOOK RAVISHING, MISTRESS.
GORGEOUS, STUNNING.
AN INCOMPARABLE VISION.

EXCELLENT.
I WANT TO LOOK MY VERY BEST...
FOR WHEN I MAKE MY FIRST IMPRESSION.
OH, HELLO.
YOU MUST BE THE OLYMPIANS, RIGHT?
THE GIRLS HAVE TOLD ME ALL ABOUT YOU.
I'M APHRODITE.

DON'T EVERYONE SPEAK ALL AT ONCE.
ZEUS, RIGHT?
I KNOW ALL ABOUT YOU.
I'M SURE YOU DO.
I'M HERA, HIS QUEEN.
YOUR ARRIVAL HAS MADE QUITE A STIR.
HAVE I JUST ARRIVED? I FEEL SOMEHOW LIKE I'VE ALWAYS BEEN HERE...
I'D SAY YOU'RE NEW. I SUSPECT WE WOULD HAVE NOTICED YOU BEFORE.

SINCE YOU'VE JUST ARRIVED, IT BEGS THE QUESTION—
WHERE DID YOU ARRIVE FROM?
I'VE BEEN AROUND. I'VE JUST BEEN...
...WAITING TO MAKE MY DEBUT.
WHICH YOU CERTAINLY DID IN THE FLASHIEST WAY POSSIBLE.
AND YOU ARE, WHAT... ZEUS'S SON?
DAUGHTER. ATHENA.
OH, MY MISTAKE.
THE HELMET— IT CONFUSED ME.
SPEAKING OF HELMETS...
YOU ARE VERY PRETTY.
WHY, THANK YOU.
YOU, TOO.

FORGIVE MY HALF BROTHER ARES—HE'S A GOD OF ACTION, AND NOT MUCH FOR WORDS.
I'M APOLLO. DELIGHTED TO MAKE YOUR ACQUAINTANCE.
THIS IS MY TWIN SISTER, ARTEMIS, AND MY AUNT, HESTIA.
IT'S INTERESTING—I CAN'T QUITE GET A READ ON YOU TWO. OR ATHENA, FOR THAT MATTER.
IT'S LIKE YOU'VE ALL SHUT YOURSELVES OFF, SOMEHOW...
YOU CAME FROM THE SEA. ARE YOU A NEREID?
AND THE PLANTS—THEY RESPOND TO YOU. ARE YOU A NYMPH?
WHY DON'T YOU TELL ME WHAT YOU THINK I AM?
THE OLYMPIANS SWARMED AROUND APHRODITE.
THE GODS FELL OVER THEMSELVES TO GET NOTICED BY THE NEW GODDESS.
THE GODDESSES BRISTLED AND CHAFED AT THIS INTERLOPER.

OF ALL THE OLYMPIANS, ZEUS KNEW BEST THE POWER OF EROS.
HE SAW THE EROS IN APHRODITE AND KNEW HOW FORMIDABLE SHE WAS.
HE SAW THE GODS JOCKEY TO BE CLOSER TO HER, A FRIENDLY RIVALRY NOW, BUT HE COULD SEE IT BLOSSOM SOON INTO FIGHTING, INTO WAR.
A WAR BETWEEN GODS. ZEUS HAD SEEN IT BEFORE. HE KNEW HOW DESTRUCTIVE IT COULD BE.
THE LAST WAR OF THE GODS HAD ENDED THE REIGN OF KRONOS.

LEFT UNCHECKED, THE POWER OF APHRODITE COULD DO THE SAME TO HIM, UNLESS...
APHRODITE! I WELCOME YOU TO THE OLYMPIANS—AS MY DAUGHTER!
DAUGHTER?
A STRANGE ROLE FOR APHRODITE, SHE WHO WAS IN A SENSE THE OLDEST OF THE ASSEMBLED GODS.
DAUGHTER? JUST WHEN I THINK HE CAN'T SURPRISE ME ANYMORE.
IT'S NOT HIS USUAL REACTION TO A PRETTY FACE, TO BE SURE...
BUT WATCH CLOSELY: HE FEELS THREATENED BY HER. HE'S MANEUVERING HER, POSITIONING HER.
AND I WANT YOU TO THINK OF ME AS YOUR FATHER.
YOU WILL COME LIVE WITH US ON MOST WONDROUS OLYMPUS, HOME OF THE GODS. YOU WILL DRINK OF OUR NECTAR, SUP OF OUR AMBROSIA...

AND OF COURSE, AS YOUR FATHER, IT FALLS TO ME TO LOOK AFTER YOUR WELL-BEING, YOUR PROTECTION, YOUR FUTURE.
YOU SEEM TO BE OF MARRIAGEABLE AGE. YOU NEED A SUITABLE HUSBAND!
HEY, I JUST GOT HERE—
YOU'LL MARRY, UH...
HIM!
MY SON HEPHAISTOS!
HIM?
HIM?
ME?
THE WEDDING OF APHRODITE AND HEPHAISTOS WAS RUSHED AND PERFUNCTORY, BUT IT SERVED ITS PURPOSE.
THE GODS WOULD NO LONGER FIGHT FOR HER HAND, NOW THAT IT WAS TIED IN MATRIMONY.
SHE WHO HAD SO MUCH LOVE TO GIVE, WHO **WAS** LOVE, WAS TRAPPED IN A LOVELESS MARRIAGE.

A HOT, SOOTY FORGE WAS NO PLACE FOR APHRODITE.
FOR HIS PART, HEPHAISTOS WAS GENTLE AND KINDHEARTED.
HE WAS ALSO, UNFORTUNATELY, COARSE, AND UNATTRACTIVE. HE WAS NOT MUCH OF A CONVERSATIONALIST. WHEN HE WALKED, HE WAS AWKWARD AND UNGAINLY.
BUT HEPHAISTOS WAS A CRAFTSMAN BEYOND COMPARE.
UGLY THOUGH HE WAS, THE THINGS HE MADE WERE BEAUTIFUL BEYOND WORDS.

ALTHOUGH HE HADN'T ASKED TO BE MARRIED TO THE LADY, HE STILL WANTED ONLY TO PLEASE HER.
BUT THE LADY HAD SO MUCH LOVE TO GIVE.
GRF.
PLEASE GIVE ME YOUR BEGUILING HAND, BELOVED. I'VE MADE SOMETHING FOR YOU.
AH.

HERE.
DO YOU LIKE IT?
YES.
THANK YOU, MY HUSBAND. IT IS VERY PRETTY.

IT'S VERY STUFFY IN HERE. I'M GOING TO GO FOR A WALK.
TAKE CARE, BELOVED!
BROTHER ARES...
I CAN'T HELP BUT NOTICE THAT YOU'VE BEEN JOINING ME IN MY FORGE MUCH MORE OFTEN OF LATE.
YOU CRAFT THE SHARPEST BLADES.
AND THERE IS NO SHORTAGE OF WARS IN THE WORLD.
POOR, POOR APHRODITE.
SO ALONE! SO UNHAPPY!
IF ONLY WE COULD DO SOMETHING FOR HER!

I SWEAR, I FEEL LIKE THOSE CYCLOPES ARE ALWAYS STARING AT ME...
LADY APHRODITE!
WE WERE JUST TALKING ABOUT YOU!
OF COURSE YOU WERE.
HOW COULD WE, THE CHARITES, HELP OUR BLESSED LADY?
MARRIED, BY THE UNBREAKABLE WILL OF ZEUS, TO HEPHAISTOS.
HEPHAISTOS, WHO WOULD RATHER SPEND HIS DAYS HUNCHED OVER A HOT FORGE THAN WITH OUR SWEET MISTRESS?
I DON'T NEED MY HUSBAND TO HAVE A GOOD TIME.

TRUE TO HER WORD, THE LADY WHO WAS LOVE HAD MANY ADVENTURES...
AND MANY LOVES.
APHRODITE MADE HERSELF A FORCE IN THE WORLD, AND WE CHARITES WERE GRACED TO BE HER COMPANIONS— TO WITNESS HER EXPLOITS.

ON CYPRUS, THE ISLAND THAT FIRST GAVE HOST TO OUR LADY, THERE LIVED A MAN.
THIS MAN, PYGMALION, MADE HIS LIVING AS A SCULPTOR. THOUGH A MORTAL, HIS ABILITY WAS NEAR DIVINE.
HIS SCULPTURES WERE SO LIFELIKE THEY ALMOST SEEMED TO BREATHE.
ALMOST.
SO GIVEN OVER WAS PYGMALION TO HIS GIFT THAT HE HAD NEVER HAD TIME TO FIND LOVE OF HIS OWN.

HE WAS LONELY, BUT NEVER REALIZED IT.
UNTIL ONE DAY, HE ACHIEVED PERFECTION.
AN IVORY STATUE OF OUR LADY, APHRODITE.
PYGMALION LOOKED UPON HIS CREATION, AND HIS HEART SWELLED WITH LOVE.
HE HAD FALLEN IN LOVE WITH AN UNLIVING STATUE.

OVER THE WEEKS TO COME, PYGMALION BEGAN TO SPEAK TO THE STATUE, IN THE MOST GENTLE AND LOVING TONES. HE BROUGHT IT GIFTS AND FLOWERS.
EACH DAY PYGMALION DRESSED THE STATUE IN DIFFERENT BEAUTIFUL ROBES.
HE ADORNED ITS DELICATE HANDS WITH ORNAMENTS AND JEWELRY.
HE APPLIED MAKEUP TO ITS FACE, UNTIL IT SEEMED ALMOST ALIVE, ALMOST BREATHING.
AT NIGHT, PYGMALION WOULD LAY THE STATUE ON A BED OF SILK SHEETS AND SOFT PILLOWS, AS IF IT NEEDED REST.
ALMOST.

THE STATUE'S IVORY EYES STARED UNBLINKING INTO THE DARKNESS.
AND PYGMALION KNEW DESPAIR.
DURING THE FEAST DAYS OF APHRODITE, PYGMALION MADE THE PILGRIMAGE TO HER TEMPLE ON THE OTHER SIDE OF THE ISLAND.
ORIGINALLY HE HAD PLANNED TO GIFT THE IVORY STATUE OF APHRODITE TO THE TEMPLE DURING THESE HIGH HOLY DAYS.

BUT NOW HE HAD A DIFFERENT PLAN.
GREETINGS TO YOU, LADY APHRODITE.
IF IT IS TRUE, O GODDESS, THAT YOU CAN GIVE ALL THINGS.
I PRAY TO YOU, TO HAVE AS MY WIFE MY IVORY STATUE-
I MEAN,
TO HAVE AS MY WIFE, ONE LIKE MY IVORY STATUE.
THE FLAMES IN A NEARBY BRAZIER LEAPED UP, AS IF THE GODDESS UNDERSTOOD.
BECAUSE, AS THE GODDESS OF LOVE, OF COURSE APHRODITE KNEW EXACTLY WHAT PYGMALION WISHED FOR. SHE PAID PYGMALION'S WORKSHOP A VISIT THAT NIGHT.

THERE SHE IS, LADY.
YES, SHE'S A BEAUTY, A WORK OF ART ALMOST WORTHY OF MY HUSBAND'S SKILLS.
SHE DOESN'T LOOK MUCH LIKE ME, REALLY, BUT I DO PREFER THE LIKENESS TO MY STATUE IN THE TEMPLE.
BREATHE, LITTLE STATUE.
PYGMALION RACED HOME. HAD THE GODDESS HEARD HIS PRAYER? HAD SHE UNDERSTOOD HIS WISH?

PYGMALION AND GALATEA (FOR THAT WAS THE NAME THE NOW-LIVING STATUE TOOK FOR HERSELF) WERE WED IN THE FALL.
IT WAS A GRAND AFFAIR, FOR PYGMALION'S GIFTS HAD MADE HIM A WEALTHY MAN, AND HE INVITED THE ENTIRE TOWN.
DURING THE RECEPTION, PYGMALION NOTICED A TALL WOMAN STANDING ALONE.
HELLO, UH, I DON'T THINK I KNOW YOU, BUT I FEEL, SOMEHOW...
LIKE WE OUGHT TO THANK YOU?
THERE IS NOTHING TO THANK ME FOR.
LOVE LIKE YOUR HUSBAND HAS IS LOVE THAT MUST BE SHARED.
BE HAPPY TOGETHER.
YOU WERE MADE FOR EACH OTHER.

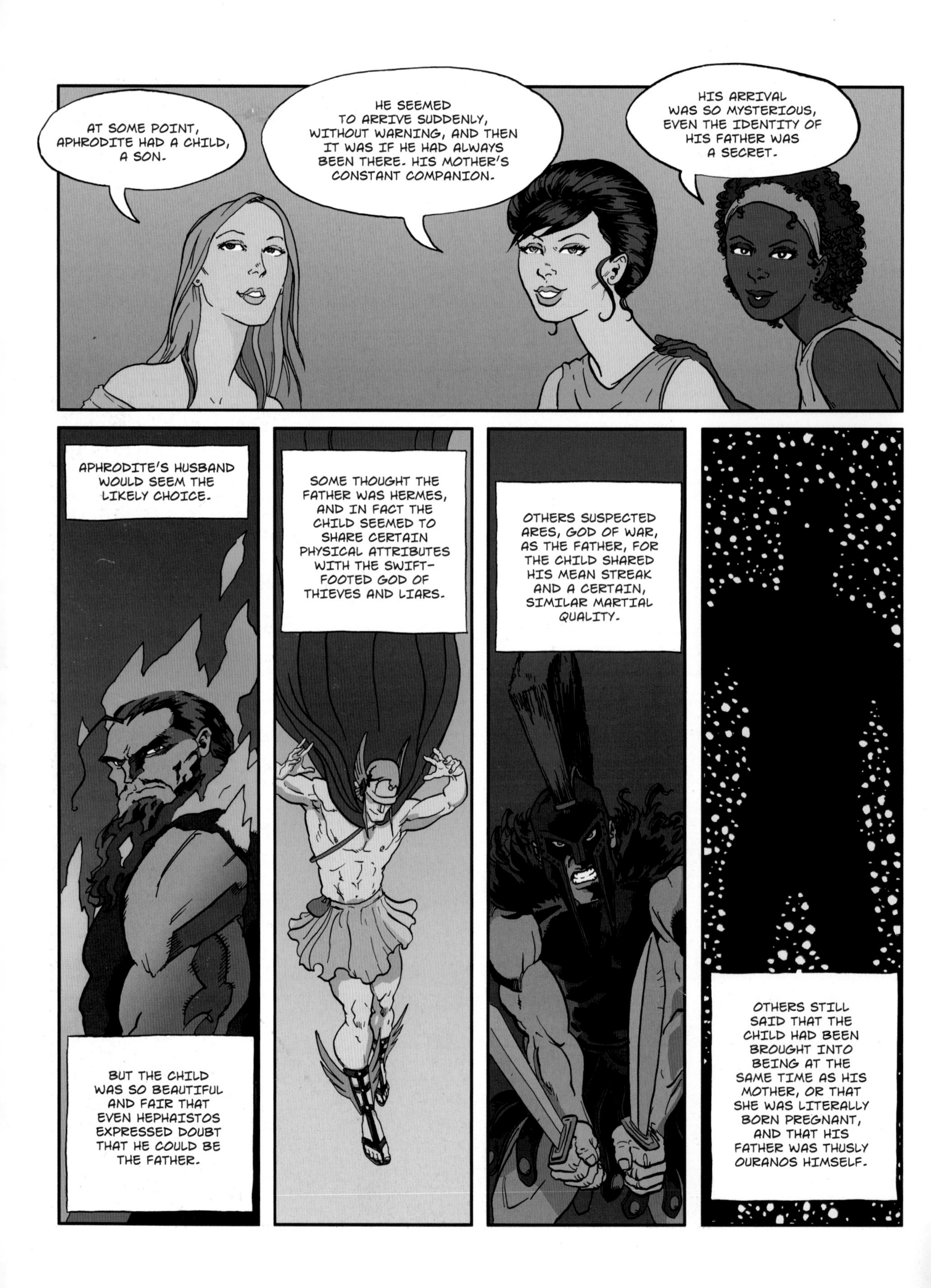
AT SOME POINT, APHRODITE HAD A CHILD, A SON.
HE SEEMED TO ARRIVE SUDDENLY, WITHOUT WARNING, AND THEN IT WAS IF HE HAD ALWAYS BEEN THERE. HIS MOTHER'S CONSTANT COMPANION.
HIS ARRIVAL WAS SO MYSTERIOUS, EVEN THE IDENTITY OF HIS FATHER WAS A SECRET.
APHRODITE'S HUSBAND WOULD SEEM THE LIKELY CHOICE.
BUT THE CHILD WAS SO BEAUTIFUL AND FAIR THAT EVEN HEPHAISTOS EXPRESSED DOUBT THAT HE COULD BE THE FATHER.
SOME THOUGHT THE FATHER WAS HERMES, AND IN FACT THE CHILD SEEMED TO SHARE CERTAIN PHYSICAL ATTRIBUTES WITH THE SWIFT-FOOTED GOD OF THIEVES AND LIARS.
OTHERS SUSPECTED ARES, GOD OF WAR, AS THE FATHER, FOR THE CHILD SHARED HIS MEAN STREAK AND A CERTAIN, SIMILAR MARTIAL QUALITY.
OTHERS STILL SAID THAT THE CHILD HAD BEEN BROUGHT INTO BEING AT THE SAME TIME AS HIS MOTHER, OR THAT SHE WAS LITERALLY BORN PREGNANT, AND THAT HIS FATHER WAS THUSLY OURANOS HIMSELF.

BUT ONE THING WAS SURE. NO MATTER WHO THE FATHER, THE BOY WAS VERY MUCH HIS MOTHER'S CHILD.
HE WAS BEAUTIFUL, AND HE DELIGHTED IN LAUGHTER JUST LIKE HER. MOREOVER, HE SHARED HER POWER TO FOMENT PASSION AND LOVE IN OTHERS AND IN THE WORLD AROUND HIM.
NATURALLY, APHRODITE NAMED HIM EROS.
THIS EROS DARTED ABOUT ON HIS WINGS OF GOLD, SOWING MISCHIEF WHEREVER HE FLEW.
HE WAS ARMED WITH A BOW, AND IN HIS QUIVER HE HAD TWO DIFFERENT TYPES OF ARROWS.
THE GOLDEN ARROWS BROUGHT LOVE TO THE HEART OF WHOMEVER THEY WOUNDED.

WHEREAS THE ARROWS OF IRON TURNED LOVE AWAY.
WHILE HIS MOTHER USED HER POWERS MORE WISELY AND DISCREETLY, YOUNG EROS USED HIS LIKE THE MERCURIAL CHILD HE WAS.

BUT IN HIS MOTHER'S
EYES, EROS COULD DO
NO WRONG.
MAN, BEAST, OR GOD,
ALL WERE POTENTIAL
TARGETS FOR THE
CAPRICIOUS YOUNG
GOD OF LOVE.
EVEN MIGHTY ZEUS FOUND
HIMSELF AT EROS'S MERCY ON
MORE THAN ONE OCCASION.

AAAOW!
WHAT WAS THAT?!
AND WHOOO...
IS THIS?
THE EYES OF AN OLYMPIAN CAN SEE WHAT THEY NEED, OR WANT TO SEE.
OH!
HEY THERE, GORGEOUS. I'M ZEUS, KING OF THE GODS.
OH, I KNOW. FUNNY, I WAS JUST THINKING ABOUT YOU...

REALLY? HAVE WE MET?
I'LL SAY. YOU MUST NOT RECOGNIZE ME.
I'M A SHAPE-SHIFTER.
I'M VERY VERSATILE.
MY LUCKY DAY!
YOU GOT THAT RIGHT. I'M THETIS.
THETIS... NOW, WHY DO I KNOW THAT NAME?
WELL, MY DAD IS THE OLD SEA GOD NEREUS...
THAT MUST BE IT...
ACTUALLY, THERE WAS ANOTHER REASON ZEUS KNEW THETIS!
IT HAD BEEN PROPHESIED THAT ANY CHILDREN OF THETIS WOULD BE TWICE AS GREAT AS THEIR FATHER!
BUT SHH! DON'T TELL ZEUS!
OOPS, LOOKS LIKE HE REMEMBERED!

TO MAKE SURE HE WOULD NEVER MAKE THIS MISTAKE AGAIN, ZEUS ARRANGED FOR THETIS TO MARRY A MORTAL NAMED PELEUS.
ANY CHILDREN OF THETIS WOULD BE FAR GREATER THAN PELEUS, BUT CONSIDERABLY LESS THAN A GOD.
ZEUS ORGANIZED THE WEDDING HIMSELF, AND EVEN COMPOSED THE GUEST LIST.

THETIS, SHE'S THE ONE WHOSE CHILD WILL BE TWICE AS GREAT AS THEIR FATHER, RIGHT? I PURSUED HER ONCE, BEFORE I REMEMBERED.
ME, TOO! THAT'S WHY I MARRIED HER OFF!

WELL, YOU DODGED THAT ARROW, ZEUS.
TELL ME ABOUT IT.
ARROW,
HMMM...
THE WEDDING OF THETIS AND PELEUS WAS A GRAND AFFAIR, AND EVERY DIVINITY WAS IN ATTENDANCE.
EVERY DIVINITY, EXCEPT ONE. ERIS, THE GODDESS OF DISCORD.
WHEREVER THERE WAS A FIGHT, AN ARGUMENT, A DISAGREEMENT, A SPAT, ERIS WAS THERE.
SMALL WONDER SHE WASN'T INVITED.
I'M SORRY, YOU'RE JUST NOT ON THE GUEST LIST—
WHY, I'LL HUFF AND I'LL—
IS THERE A PROBLEM HERE?
THEY SAY I'M NOT INVITED!
I'M SURE IT'S JUST AN OVERSIGHT. I CAN VOUCH FOR HER.
AND YOU WILL BE ON YOUR BEST BEHAVIOR, WON'T YOU, ERIS?
HMMF

BUT ERIS WAS OFFENDED, AND SHE WAS GOING TO MAKE SURE EVERYONE KNEW IT.
SHE WANDERED FROM SEAT TO SEAT, JUMPING UP AND SQUAWKING LOUDLY AT RANDOM INTERVALS.
SHE SANG TUNELESSLY, AND BANGED LOUDLY ON A SHIELD UNTIL ARES STOPPED HER.
THEN, SHE TRIED TO CREATE A FIRE UNTIL HEPHAISTOS MADE HER CEASE.
ERIS SAT AWHILE IN AN ANGRY SULK, TRYING TO FIGURE OUT HOW SHE MIGHT SOMEHOW FREE THE TITANS AND DISRUPT THE WEDDING.
THEN SHE HAD THE BEST IDEA SHE'D EVER HAD IN HER LIFE.
HEY!

FOR THE MOST BEAUTIFUL ONE!
SHE WOUND UP AND THREW—
—A BEAUTIFUL GOLDEN APPLE, LIKE THE ONES FROM HERA'S OWN GARDEN OF HESPERIDES.
HEE HOO HEE HA HO

AWK-WARD.
WELL, WHAT SHALL WE DO NOW? APPARENTLY WE ALL FEEL WE'RE ENTITLED...
I SUPPOSE YOU THINK IT SHOULD JUST GO TO YOU. YOU OBVIOUSLY FEEL YOU'RE THE MOST BEAUTIFUL.
YOU SAID IT, HONEY, NOT ME.
EVIDENTLY WE ALL FEEL WE'RE THE MOST BEAUTIFUL, OR WE WOULDN'T BE HERE HAVING HIS CONVERSATION.

YEAH, AND ISN'T THAT A BIT OUT OF CHARACTER FOR YOU? SINCE WHEN DO YOU CARE ABOUT YOUR LOOKS?
I CARE VERY MUCH ABOUT MY APPEARANCE! JUST BECAUSE I DON'T DRESS LIKE A FLOOZY—
OH, A CUTTING REMARK FROM PALLAS ATHENA! I KNOW IT WAS DIRECTED AT ME BECAUSE I'M THE ONLY ONE HERE NOT DRESSED LIKE A SOLDIER OR A FRUMP!
WHAT IS THAT SUPPOSED TO MEAN? ARE YOU SAYING I DRESS UNFASHIONABLY?
IF THE SANDAL FITS, HERA.
MAYBE IF YOU CUT LOOSE EVERY ONCE IN A WHILE, YOUR HUSBAND—
ZEUS!
WHAT'S GOING ON HERE?
WE NEED YOU TO SETTLE SOMETHING!
WHICHEVER ONE OF US IS THE MOST BEAUTIFUL GETS THIS AP-
-PLE.
THAT'S NOT YOURS.

HOW DARE YOU— I KNOW—

KRAK
AS THE KING OF GODS, IT FELL TO ZEUS TO SETTLE DISPUTES AMONG THE OLYMPIANS.
BUT HE WASN'T STUPID.
LADIES, YOU ARE ALL SO BEAUTIFUL TO ME—
I COULDN'T POSSIBLY JUDGE.

TO CHOOSE BETWEEN MY LOVELY WIFE AND DAUGHTERS? INCONCEIVABLE!
AGAIN WITH THE DAUGHTER THING...
A JUDGE MUST BE IMPARTIAL.
AND SO, I FIND I MUST APPOINT A NEW JUDGE TO DECIDE WHICH OF YOU BEAUTIFUL LADIES IS THE MOST FAIR...
SAY ANYONE BUT HERMES ANYONE BUT HERMES ANYONE BUT HERMES...
HERMES!
HA!
POP, YOU'RE KILLING ME HERE.
WORRY NOT, SON! ON THE SLOPES OF MOUNT IDA, THERE IS A SHEPHERD. HIS NAME IS PARIS. FIND HIM, FOR IT WILL FALL TO HIM TO DECIDE WHICH OF THESE THREE IS MOST BEAUTIFUL.
A MORTAL SHEPHERD? TO JUDGE THREE GODDESSES? I'M THE GOD OF LIARS FOR A REASON, POP. WHAT'S YOUR GAME HERE?
WELL, HE IS SECRETLY A PRINCE OF TROY...
YOU KNOW WHAT? I DON'T THINK I WANT TO KNOW.
YOU CAN TRUST ME.
SHYEAH, RIGHT, AND I'M A CYCLOPS...

AND SURE ENOUGH, ON THE SLOPES OF MOUNT IDA...
NICELY PLAYED.
PERSONALLY, I PREFER THE LYRE, BUT I'VE ALWAYS HAD A SOFT SPOT FOR SHEPHERD'S MUSIC.
REMINDS ME OF MY YOUTH.
LORD HERMES!
NO TIME FOR THAT, WE HAVE A LOT TO DO—IT TURNS OUT YOU'RE A PRINCE OF TROY.
AND THAT'S JUST THE START OF YOUR GOOD NEWS TODAY.
YOU ARE BEAUTY WITHOUT COMPARE, MILADY. YOU KNOW THIS.
BUT THIS CONTEST, MILADY. I—WE FIND IT...
IT IS BENEATH YOU, MILADY.

BENEATH ME?
WE ARE SO SORRY, MISTRESS!
WE DIDN'T MEAN—
WE ONLY WANTED—
NO, YOU ARE RIGHT. TO BE JUDGED BY A MORTAL, EVEN A PRINCE? THIS IS BENEATH ME, BENEATH US ALL.
AND YET, WHY DO I CARE, WHY DO I SUBJECT MYSELF TO THIS CONTEST?
ATHENA IS A BORN WARRIOR. HERA IS PURE POWER—SHE IS, AFTER ALL, THE QUEEN OF THE GODS. I HAVE NO SUCH WEAPONS.
MY WEAPON, SUCH AS IT IS, IS ONLY MY GRACE, MY CHARM, MY GIFT OF SEDUCTION. A POWERFUL ABILITY, TO BE SURE, BUT CAN IT STAND AGAINST SUCH POWER AS ATHENA AND HERA WIELD?
IF I CANNOT WIN THIS CONTEST BASED ON MY CHARMS, WHAT DOES IT SAY OF MY PLACE AMONG THE GODS?

—SO, YEAH, YOU'RE THE SON OF KING PRIAM OF TROY. BECAUSE OF A PROPHECY, YOU WERE LEFT EXPOSED ON A MOUNTAIN, WHERE YOU WERE PROTECTED AND FED BY, OF ALL THINGS, A SHE-BEAR.
EVENTUALLY, YOU WERE ADOPTED BY THE SHEPHERD AGELAUS AND RAISED AS HIS SON. AND NOW HERE YOU ARE!
IT'S A LOT TO TAKE IN ALL AT ONCE, BUT DON'T WORRY—YOU'LL FORGET ALL ABOUT IT SOON ENOUGH, AND ONLY REMEMBER IT LATER. THAT'S HOW THIS DIVINE REVELATION THING WORKS.
T-THIS IS A LOT TO WRAP MY HEAD AROUND...
BUT ENOUGH OF THAT. SEE THIS APPLE? VERY PRETTY, YES?
UHM, YES—
THAT'S RIGHT, IT IS. AND YOU, YOU LUCKY, LUCKY MAN, YOU GET TO DECIDE WHO GETS TO KEEP IT!
BY DECIDING WHO IS THE MOST BEAUTIFUL GODDESS!
GODDESS?
AND WITHOUT FURTHER ADO...

I AM HERA, QUEEN OF THE GODS AND SOVEREIGN OF THE HEAVENS. I HAVE NO NEED TO PROVE MY BEAUTY, FOR AM I NOT THE BRIDE OF ALMIGHTY ZEUS HIMSELF?
ABSOLUTE POWER IS MINE. CHOOSE WISELY IN THIS CONTEST, AND AS RULER OF ALL I CAN SEE I WILL LOOK KINDLY UPON YOU.
I UNDERSTAND THAT YOU ARE A PRINCE OF TROY. WITH MY INFLUENCE, YOU WILL BE KING. AND NOT JUST OF TROY, BUT ALL OF ASIA.
UNTOLD RICHES, MARVELS, AND PEOPLE— ENTIRE CULTURES YOU'VE NEVER DREAMED OF— UNITED UNDER YOUR MIGHTY RULE.
THAT, PARIS, IS WHAT I CAN OFFER.

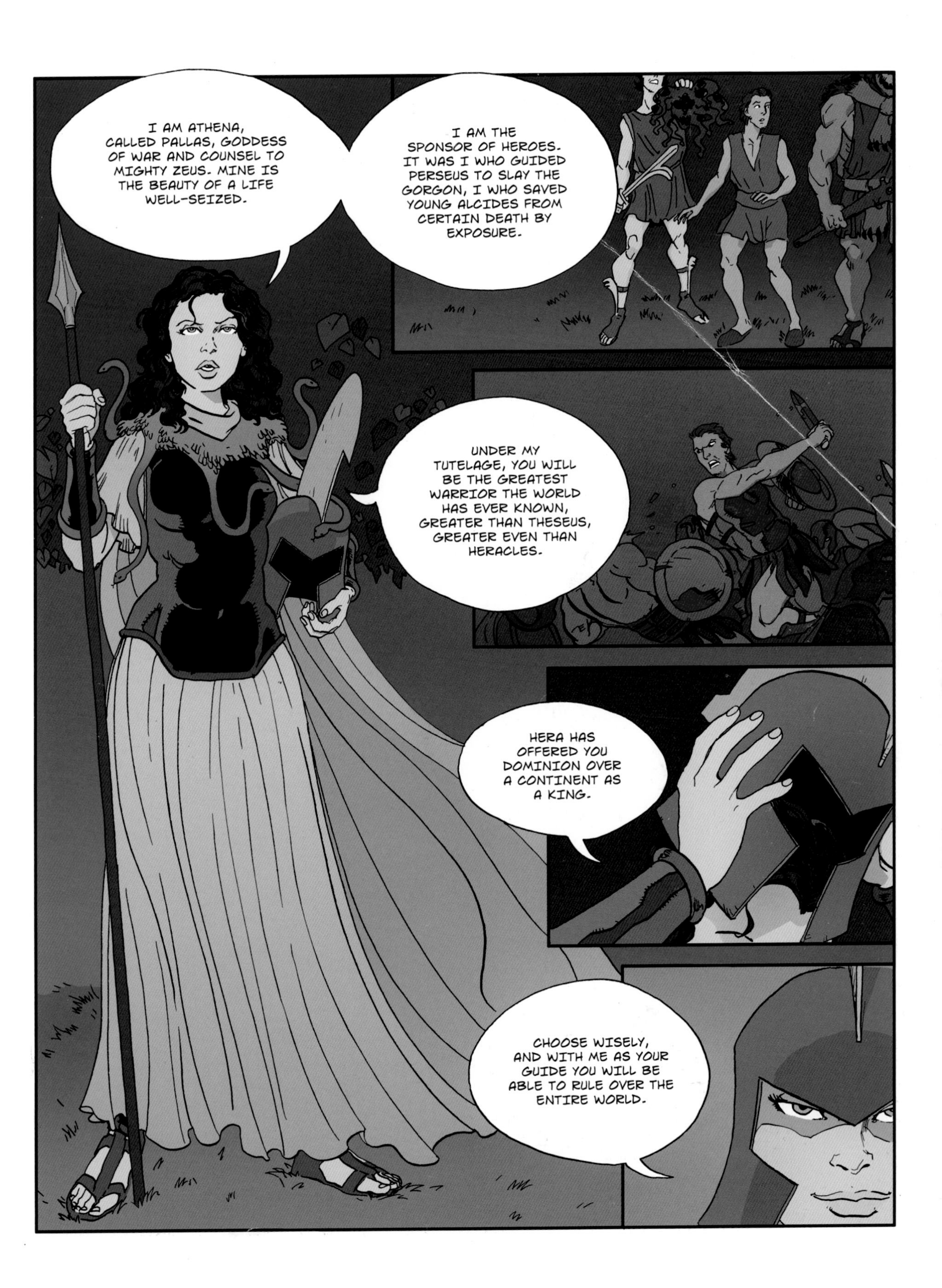
I AM ATHENA, CALLED PALLAS, GODDESS OF WAR AND COUNSEL TO MIGHTY ZEUS. MINE IS THE BEAUTY OF A LIFE WELL-SEIZED.
I AM THE SPONSOR OF HEROES. IT WAS I WHO GUIDED PERSEUS TO SLAY THE GORGON, I WHO SAVED YOUNG ALCIDES FROM CERTAIN DEATH BY EXPOSURE.
UNDER MY TUTELAGE, YOU WILL BE THE GREATEST WARRIOR THE WORLD HAS EVER KNOWN, GREATER THAN THESEUS, GREATER EVEN THAN HERACLES.
HERA HAS OFFERED YOU DOMINION OVER A CONTINENT AS A KING.
CHOOSE WISELY, AND WITH ME AS YOUR GUIDE YOU WILL BE ABLE TO RULE OVER THE ENTIRE WORLD.

AND MY GREETINGS TO YOU, NEWLY MINTED MORTAL PRINCE.
HERA HAS OFFERED YOU POLITICAL POWER, ATHENA POWER IN WAR.
BUT I KNOW WHAT MEN LIKE YOU REALLY WANT.
A WOMAN, JUST LIKE ME.
I AM APHRODITE, GODDESS OF BEAUTY AND LOVE, BORN OF THE SEA, THE MOTHER OF DESIRE.

MINE IS THE VERY POWER TO GIVE LIFE ITSELF—THE POWER THAT RULES BOTH MEN AND GODS.
CHOOSE ME AND TURN DOWN THE SCEPTER OF ASIA—ACCEPT MY BEAUTY AND FORGET WAR.
IN PLACE OF THOSE MANLY PURSUITS, WITH MY GUIDANCE YOU SHALL HAVE THE LOVE OF THE MOST BEAUTIFUL WOMAN IN THE WORLD.
ASK YOURSELF—AM I NOT THE MOST FAIR, BY FAR?
CHOOSE WISELY, MY HANDSOME PRINCELING.

WELL, WHO DO YOU CHOOSE, PARIS?

HER.
I CHOOSE HER!

AND THAT'S THAT, THE CHOICE IS MADE! THANKS FOR COMING, ONE AND ALL!

AND FOR YOU, MIGHTY APHRODITE.

THE GOLDEN APPLE GOES TO THE MOST BEAUTIFUL ONE.

THANK YOU. IT'S VERY PRETTY.
YOU... YOU JUST THREW IT AWAY?
WHAT WAS THE POINT OF OUR DEBASING OURSELVES LIKE THIS?!
HONEY, IF YOU HAVE TO ASK...
WHAT A GODDE— OOF!

LADY APHRODITE?
YOU PROMISED ME THE LOVE OF THE MOST BEAUTIFUL WOMAN IN THE WORLD?
OH, YES. DO YOU KNOW WHO THE MOST BEAUTIFUL WOMAN IN THE WORLD IS, PARIS?
I DO NOT.
HER NAME IS HELEN, AND SHE IS MARRIED TO KING MENELAUS OF SPARTA.
SHE'S NOT QUITE AS BEAUTIFUL AS ME, BUT BY MORTAL STANDARDS SHE IS QUITE BEWITCHING.
SHE IS EXQUISITE!
WHEN DO I GET HER?
I'M NOT GOING TO GIVE HER TO YOU, SILLY MAN.
SHE IS A PERSON, NOT A GOLDEN TRINKET.
WHAT I WILL GIVE YOU IS LOVE IN YOUR HEART FOR HER.
THIS LOVE WILL MAKE YOU CONTEST FOR HER, AND PROVE YOURSELF WORTHY OF HER.

YOU ARE A PRINCE OF TROY NOW.
GO FORTH, PARIS, CLAIM YOUR BIRTHRIGHT, AND USE YOUR NEW STATUS TO WIN THE HEART OF HELEN.
YOU SENT HIM OFF TO SEDUCE A WOMAN WHO'S ALREADY MARRIED TO ANOTHER.
BEING THE GODDESS OF MARRIAGE, MAYBE I'M BIASED...
BUT IT WOULD SEEM YOU DON'T RESPECT THE INSTITUTION OF MARRIAGE AT ALL.
I BELIEVE MARRIAGE IS A CELEBRATION OF TWO SOULS UNITED IN LOVE
AND NOT A POLITICAL UNION OF CONVENIENCE.
THAT SORT OF INSTITUTION DESERVES TO BE TORN DOWN.

I'M NOT PROUD OF HOW WE ALL BEHAVED...
BUT I DON'T THINK YOU MADE ANY FRIENDS HERE TODAY.
I DON'T THINK I MADE MANY FRIENDS HERE, WHEN I FIRST CAME OUT OF THE SEA, ALL THOSE YEARS AGO...
YOU MAY BE RIGHT ABOUT THAT, ALAS.
SO, UH, YOU DOING ANYTHING LATER?
I DON'T THINK SO, HERMES.
OH WELL, YOU KNOW WHERE TO FIND ME!

MOTHER! MOTHER! OH, I AM DYING!
I HAVE BEEN KILLED! KILLED!
EROS, WHAT ARE YOU GOING ON ABOUT?
I WAS HIDING IN THE FLOWERS OVER THERE, AND I WAS BITTEN! BITTEN BY A TINY WINGED SERPENT!
IT WAS JUST A BEE, EROS.
OH, BUT IT STINGS MOTHER!
IF A BEE STING IS SO PAINFUL, EROS, WHAT PAIN DO YOU SUPPOSE OUR VICTIMS SUFFER?
NOW COME, LET US GO BACK TO OLYMPUS. WE'LL FIND SOMETHING FOR THE HURT...

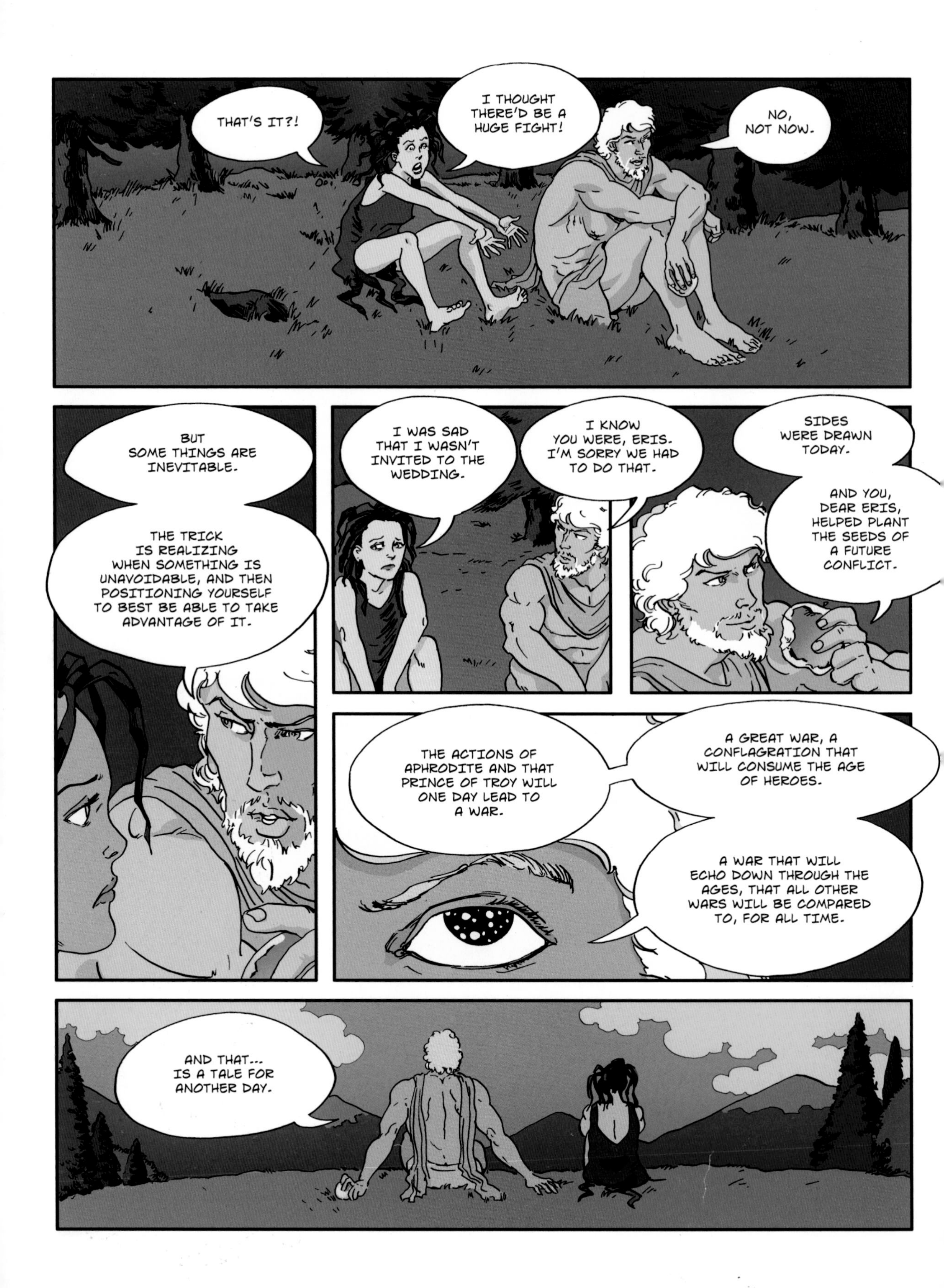
THAT'S IT?!
I THOUGHT THERE'D BE A HUGE FIGHT!
NO, NOT NOW.
BUT SOME THINGS ARE INEVITABLE.
THE TRICK IS REALIZING WHEN SOMETHING IS UNAVOIDABLE, AND THEN POSITIONING YOURSELF TO BEST BE ABLE TO TAKE ADVANTAGE OF IT.
I WAS SAD THAT I WASN'T INVITED TO THE WEDDING.
I KNOW YOU WERE, ERIS. I'M SORRY WE HAD TO DO THAT.
SIDES WERE DRAWN TODAY.
AND YOU, DEAR ERIS, HELPED PLANT THE SEEDS OF A FUTURE CONFLICT.
THE ACTIONS OF APHRODITE AND THAT PRINCE OF TROY WILL ONE DAY LEAD TO A WAR.
A GREAT WAR, A CONFLAGRATION THAT WILL CONSUME THE AGE OF HEROES.
A WAR THAT WILL ECHO DOWN THROUGH THE AGES, THAT ALL OTHER WARS WILL BE COMPARED TO, FOR ALL TIME.
AND THAT... IS A TALE FOR ANOTHER DAY.

CHARITES
ATTENDANTS OF APHRODITE

GODDESSES OF Grace, Beauty, Adornment

ROMAN NAME The Gratiae

INDIVIDUAL NAMES Aglaia ("Glory"), Euphrosyne ("Merriment"), Thalia ("Festivity")

HEAVENLY BODIES The asteroid Charis is named after the Charites; each of the individual Charites also has an asteroid named after her.

SACRED PLACES Boeotia, the oldest site of their worship in ancient Greece

MODERN LEGACY Such modern words as charity, charisma, and grace are derived from the names of the Charites.

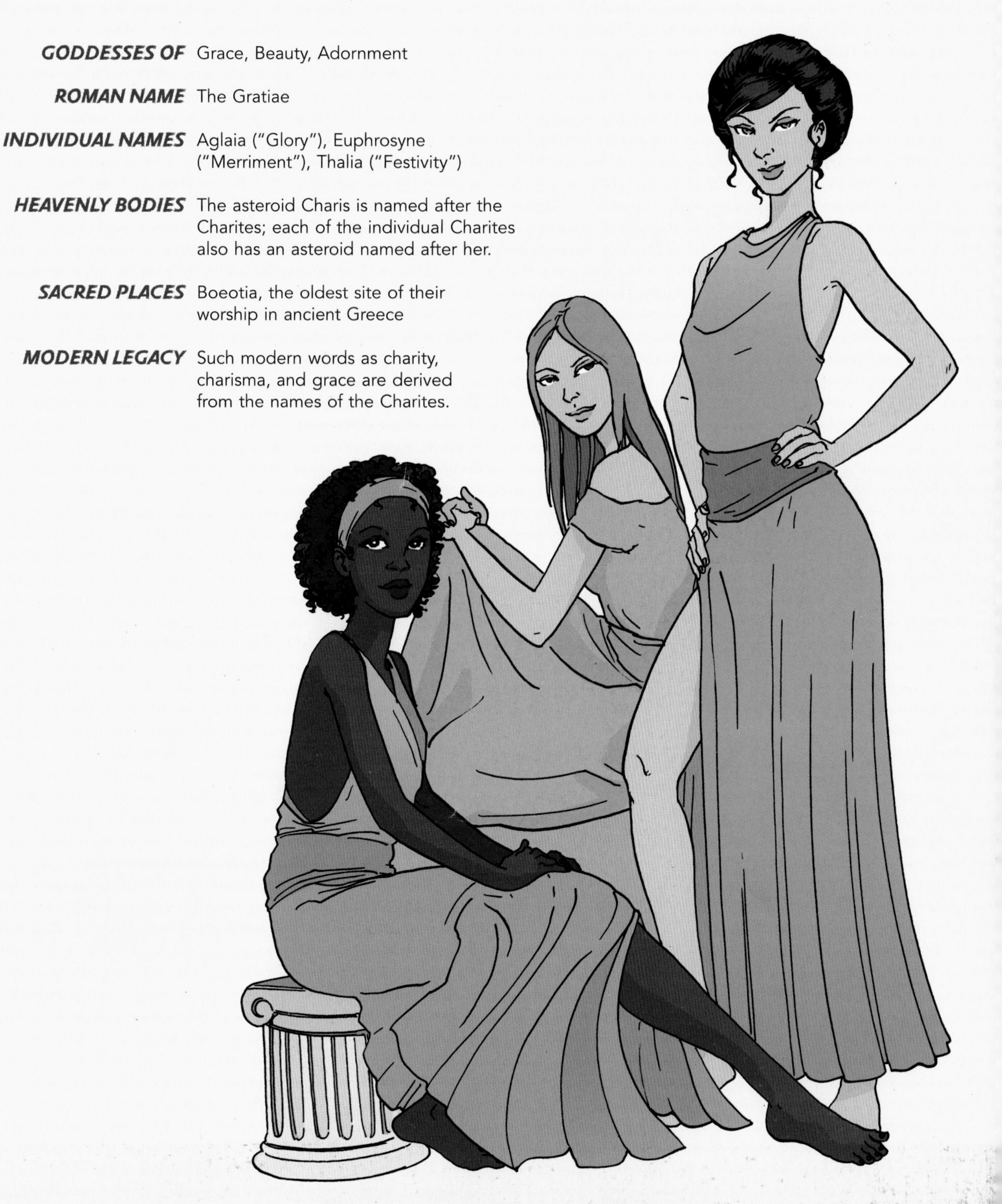

BIBLIOGRAPHY

HESIOD: VOLUME 1, THEOGENY. WORKS AND DAYS: TESTIMONIA.
NEW YORK: LOEB CLASSICAL LIBRARY, 2007.
The birth of Aphrodite from sea foam is told in many ancient sources, but Hesiod's is the version that they all draw upon.

OPPIAN, COLLUTHUS, TRYPHIODORUS. ***NEW YORK: LOEB CLASSICAL LIBRARY, 1928.***
This book is a collection of the surviving works of the three authors after whom it is named. My retelling of the Judgment of Paris owes a lot to the version that Colluthus recounts here.

OVID. METAMORPHOSES ***NEW YORK: PENGUIN CLASSICS, 2004.***
Actually a Roman text, so the gods all sport their Roman names, but this is the source I used for the story of Pygmalion.

THEOI GREEK MYTHOLOGY WEB SITE ***WWW.THEOI.COM***
Without a doubt, the single most valuable resource I came across in this entire venture. At theoi.com, you can find an encyclopedia of various gods and goddesses from Greek mythology, cross referenced with every mention of them they could find in literally hundreds of ancient Greek and Roman texts. Unfortunately, it's not quite complete, and it doesn't seem to be updated anymore.

MYTH INDEX WEB SITE ***WWW.MYTHINDEX.COM***
Another mythology Web site connected to Theoi.com. While it doesn't have the painstakingly compiled quotations from ancient texts, it does offer some impressive encyclopedic entries on virtually every character to ever pass through a Greek myth. Pretty amazing.

ALSO RECOMMENDED

FOR YOUNGER READERS

D'Aulaires' Book of Greek Myths. Ingri and Edgar Parin D'Aulaire. New York: Doubleday, 1962

We Goddesses: Athena, Aphrodite, Hera. Doris Orgel, illustrated by Marilee Heyer. New York: DK Publishing, 1999

FOR OLDER READERS

The Marriage of Cadmus and Harmony. Robert Calasso. New York: Knopf, 1993

Mythology. Edith Hamilton. New York: Grand Central Publishing, 1999

EROS

MISCHIEVOUS GODLING OF LOVE

ROMAN NAME	Cupid, Amor
SYMBOLS	His bow and arrows, a flaming torch
SACRED PLACES	Thespiae, one of the comparatively few cities where Eros had a temple not shared with his mother
HEAVENLY BODY	Cupid, a moon of Uranus; also 433 Eros, a near-Earth asteroid
MODERN LEGACY	Eros is still a familiar sight every February fourteenth, on Valentine's Day. As Cupid, he is one of that holiday's most prominent symbols.

To the Goddess of Love herself—thank you for letting me find Arta.
—G.O.

New York

Published by First Second
First Second is an imprint of Roaring Brook Press,
a division of Holtzbrinck Publishing Holdings Limited Partnership
175 Fifth Avenue, New York, New York 10010

Cataloging-in-Publication Data is on file at the Library of Congress

Paperback ISBN: 978-1-59643-739-5
Hardcover ISBN: 978-1-59643-947-4

First Second books may be purchased for business or promotional use.
For information on bulk purchases please contact Macmillan Corporate
and Premium Sales Department at (800) 221-7945 x5442 or by email at
specialmarkets@macmillan.com.

First Edition 2014

Cover design by Colleen AF Venable
Book design by Rob Steen

Printed in China by Toppan Leefung Printing Ltd., Dongguan City, Guangdong Province

10 9 8 7 6 5 4 3 2